THE TWELVE PRINCESSES

GORDON FITCHETT

PHYLLIS FOGELMAN BOOKS

NEW YORK

There was once
a lucky king and a queen
who had twelve beautiful daughters.

All twelve of them slept in one room; and when they went to bed the doors were locked up and barred; but every morning there were their shoes worn right through as if they had been danced in all night long.

But nobody could find out
exactly what had happened, or
where the princesses had been.

So the king made it known to all the land that if any prince could discover where the princesses went at night, he could have the one he liked best for his wife, and would inherit the kingdom; but whoever tried and did not succeed after three days and nights would be put to death.

A prince soon came.

There was a special dinner for him, and in the evening he was taken to the alcove next to the chamber where the princesses lay in their twelve beds.

There he was to sit and watch where they went, so that nothing could happen without his hearing it.

But the prince soon fell asleep; and when he woke in the morning, he found their shoes—and they were full of holes.

The same thing happened the second and third nights, so the king ordered his head to be cut off.

After him came several others, but they all had the same luck, and all lost their lives in the same manner.

Now, an old soldier, who had been wounded in battle and could fight no longer, passed through the country where this king reigned. He met an old woman who asked him where he was going.

"I hardly know where I'm going, or what to do," said the soldier. "But I think I would like to find out what it is that the princesses do at night, and then in time I might be a king."

"Well," said the woman, "that's easy. Just be careful not to drink any of the wine that one of the princesses will bring you in the evening, and the moment she leaves, pretend to be fast asleep.

"See this cloak?" she said. "It will make you invisible, and you will be able to follow the princesses wherever they go." The soldier decided to try his luck. So he went to the king and said he was willing to take the challenge.

He was as well received as the others had been, with the king ordering fine royal robes to be given to him, and when the evening came, he was led to the alcove. Just as he was going to lie down, the eldest daughter brought him a cup of wine. But the soldier threw it away secretly, and soon began to snore as loudly as if he was fast asleep. The twelve princesses laughed heartily; and the eldest said, "This fellow will go the way of the others!"

So they took out all their fine clothes, and dressed themselves and skipped about as if they could not wait to get going.

But the youngest said, "You are all so happy, yet I feel very uneasy; I'm sure something terrible is going to happen."

"You simpleton," said the eldest, "you are always afraid. Have you forgotten how many princes have already watched us in vain? And this soldier is so old, even if I had not given him his sleeping draft, he would soon have been dead to the world."

When they were all ready, they went and looked at the soldier, but he snored on, and did not stir hand or foot. So they thought they were quite safe.

The eldest went up to her own bed and clapped her hands, and a trapdoor flew open. The soldier saw them going through the trapdoor one after another and, thinking he had no time to lose, he jumped up and followed them.

But in his haste he trod on the gown of the youngest princess, and she cried out to her sisters, "Things are not right: Someone took hold of my gown!"

"You silly creature!" said the eldest. "It was just a nail on the stairs."

Down they all went, and at the bottom found themselves in a grove of trees so delightful, it would be hard to imagine. The leaves were all of silver, and glittered and sparkled beautifully.

The soldier wished to take away some token of the place,
so he broke off a twig, and there came a loud noise from the tree.
At once the youngest daughter said again, "I am sure things are not
right—did you hear that noise? That's never happened before."

But the eldest said, "It is only our princes, who are shouting for
joy at our approach."

Then they came to another grove of trees, where all the leaves were of gold; and afterward to a third, where the leaves were all of glittering diamonds. The soldier broke a twig from each, and every time, there was a loud noise, which made the youngest sister tremble with fear. But the eldest still said it was only the princes, who were crying for joy.

At the edge of a great lake there stood twelve little boats with twelve handsome princes in them, who seemed to be waiting.

Each princess went into a boat, and the soldier stepped into the same boat as the youngest.

As they were rowing over the lake, the prince who was in the boat with the youngest princess and the soldier said, "I do not know why it is, but though I am rowing with all my might, we are not moving as fast as usual, and I am quite tired. The boat seems very heavy today."

"It is only the heat of the weather," said the princess. "I feel uncomfortable too."

On the other side of the lake stood a brightly lit castle, from which came the merry music of horns and trumpets. There they all landed, and went up the stairs, and each prince danced with his princess.

And the soldier, who was all the time invisible, danced with them too.

The youngest sister was still terribly frightened, but the eldest always silenced her.

They danced on till three in the morning, and then all their shoes were worn out, so they had to stop.

The princes headed back again over the lake (but this time the soldier placed himself in the boat with the eldest princess) and on the opposite shore they said their good-byes, the princesses promising to come again the following night.

When they came to the trapdoor, the soldier ran on ahead, and lay down; and as the twelve sisters dragged themselves up the stairs, they heard him snoring and thought their secret was safe.

Then they undressed, put away their fine clothes, pulled off their shoes, and went to sleep.

In the morning the soldier said nothing but, wanting to see more of this strange adventure, went again the second and third nights. And everything happened just as before: The princesses danced till their shoes were worn to pieces, and then returned home. However, on the third night the soldier carried away one of the golden cups from the palace where the princesses danced, to prove where he had been.

When the time came for him to expose their secret, he was taken before the king with the three twigs and the golden cup; and the twelve princesses stood listening behind the curtains to hear what he would say. And when the king asked, "What do my twelve daughters do all night?" he answered, "They dance with twelve princes in a castle across the lake."

And then he told the king all that had happened, and showed him the twigs and the cup.

So the king called for the princesses, and asked them whether what the soldier had said was true. And when they saw it was no use denying what had happened, they confessed everything.

Then the king asked the soldier which of them he would choose for his wife; and he answered, "I am not very young, so I will have the eldest." They were married that very day. And whether there was any more dancing for the eldest princess, who can say? For this tired, brave, clever soldier was chosen to be the next king.

THE TWELVE PRINCESSES

To Mike, Yann, Francesca, Terry, Brenda,
Paul, Nanna, ManTim, and Obe.

—G.F.

First published in the United States 2000
by Phyllis Fogelman Books
An imprint of Penguin Putnam Books for Young Readers
345 Hudson Street
New York, New York 10014

Originally published in Australia as *The Twelve Princesses* by Gordon Fitchett
Copyright © 2000 by Gordon Fitchett
This edition published by arrangement with Random House Australia
through International Horizons Pty Ltd.
All rights reserved
Jacket design by Julie Rauer
Printed in Hong Kong
First Edition
1 3 5 7 9 10 8 6 4 2

Library of Congress Cataloging in Publication Data
Fitchett, Gordon.
The twelve princesses/retold and illustrated by Gordon Fitchett.
p. cm.
Summary: retells the traditional tale in which the king's twelve daughters
wear out their shoes every night while they are supposedly sleeping in their locked bedrooms.
Illustrations show the characters depicted as ducks.
ISBN 0-8037-2474-8 (trade)
[1. Fairy tales. 2. Folklore—Germany.] I. Zertanzten schuhe.
English. II. Title. III. Title: 12 princesses.
PZ8.F5757Tw 1999 398.2'0943'02—dc21 [E] 98-45380 CIP AC

The art for this book was prepared by using colored pencils.